The Tome of Terrible Truths

Other Forgotten Fairytales Works by William Moore:

Books

The Grimoire of Forgotten Fairytales
The Book of Bitter Ends

Audio

The Grimoire Diaries

www.forgottenfairytales.com

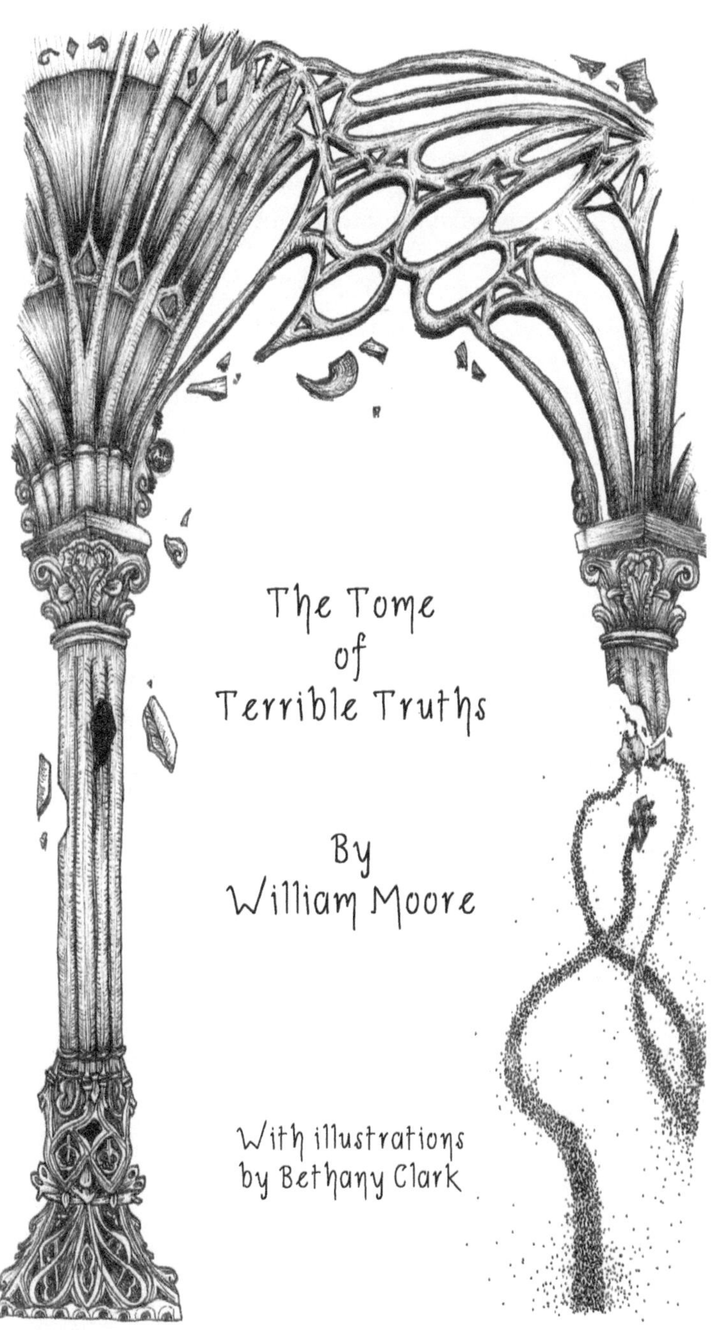

The Tome of Terrible Truths

By
William Moore

With illustrations
by Bethany Clark

www.williammooremusic.com

For permissions contact:
info@williammooremusic.com

Cover and Illustrations by Bethany Clark.

Published by Precipice.

Hardback ISBN: 978-1-7395164-4-4

For everyone whose belief holds
the power to bring dreams to life.

For Alan and Christine,
who gave me the chance to dream.

For Andrew,
whose words were a light to so many.

Editor's Note

It is with no small measure of intrigue and apprehension that I introduce this sequel to "The Grimoire of Forgotten Fairytales." A mysterious, unmarked package appeared at our office one dreary morning, its contents revealing a cache of manuscripts bearing William Moore's unmistakable handwriting. They seemed to align with his previous work, leading us to believe that they might indeed be missing pages from his enigmatic collection.

Despite our best efforts to identify the sender or ascertain the provenance of these documents, we remain in the dark. Who could have known of these writings, and why did they choose to share them now? We implore anyone with knowledge about these circumstances to come forward and shed light on this mystery.

Given the public's fervent interest in "The Grimoire of Forgotten Fairytales," we felt compelled once again to publish this new collection as it arrived. We believe it is likely the continuation of Moore's unfinished legacy, and can't help but wonder if there is more of this story to be discovered. While we still cannot verify the authenticity of these documents beyond the stylistic echoes of William's own hand, the decision to publish "The Tome of Terrible Truths" was made in earnest.

The mystery surrounding William's disappearance deepens with these pages, and I hope that as you explore this new work, you will uncover some of the answers we so desperately seek. May you approach it with the same cautious curiosity with which we present it to you.

Sincerely,

Edmund Berringer
Editor

Contents

Foreword

As I sit here tonight, with the candle's light flickering weakly against the encroaching darkness, I'm gripped by a strange blend of fear and excitement. It's a feeling I've grown accustomed to - a pull that both terrifies and draws me deeper into this strange and twisted journey. The silence around me feels almost alive, and my thoughts, uninvited, wander into the unknown, where the lines between what's real and what's imagined blur.

I can't help but think back to a time when life was simpler, before all this began. Those days feel distant now, filled with the comforts of routine and the bliss of not knowing what lay beneath the surface. But that part of me, the part that longs for that old, peaceful life, is growing quieter. In its place is a new voice - one that's drawn to the thrill of discovery, to the dark secrets hidden in the shadows of our world. It's as if I've tasted something forbidden, something so strange and compelling that I can't stop seeking more. Sometimes, in the rare quiet moments, I wonder what drives me forward. Is it just curiosity? A desire to learn more? Or is there something deeper at play - an urge to explore the mysterious and the unknown, to uncover things that perhaps should stay buried?

Each time I find a new clue, solve a riddle, or decipher a hidden message, it feels like more than just progress. It feels like I'm uncovering a truth that has always been waiting for me, something that speaks to a part of me I didn't know existed.

But there's also a fear that lingers in the back of my mind. With each step I take into the unknown, I feel like I'm walking a fine line between discovery and madness, between finding answers and losing myself. The danger is real, and the stakes are high - what happened to Harriet is a constant reminder of that. I can't shake the feeling there is a darker, grander plan at work here.

So, in these quiet hours, I write this as a way to make sense of it all. Despite the fear, despite the sleepless nights and the shadows that seem to follow me, I can't turn back. This journey has a hold on me, promising answers to questions I didn't even know I had, leading me to places I never imagined existed.

Maybe it's foolish to keep going, to chase after these dark mysteries, to risk everything for the sake of knowledge. But there's something about it that I can't resist, something that keeps me on this path. I am both the seeker and the one being pursued, searching for truths in a world filled with ancient secrets. And so, I continue, because turning back would mean denying a part of myself that I've only just begun to understand - a part that has been waiting for this moment, hidden just beneath the surface.

In the end, maybe this journey isn't just about finding hidden knowledge, but about discovering something much more personal - my own place in this vast and mysterious world. And however dangerous that place might be, it feels like it's where I'm meant to be.

In the heart of a forest, deep and wide,
Stands a temple of pillars, forty beside.

From this sacred grove, magick flows,
A hidden power the world scarcely knows.

Each pillar tall, a guardian stands,
Housing a hero from distant lands.

Spirits of valour, wisdom, and might,
Watch over the temple through day and night.

Their essence imbued in ancient stone,
A legacy of power, their eternal throne.

Whispers of enchantment drift through the air,
A testament to the strength they bear.

In the temple's shadow, mysteries unfold,
Stories of heroes, brave and bold.

Their magick feeds the forest's heart,
Binding all with their eternal art.

They are the pillars of the rising sun,
Their names are carved beneath each one:

Ôn Lệ Hương

Mark James Bowery

Teaisha Marie

Edward Arthur Flint

Katherine Ann King

Izzy Chloris

Marc Leo

Samuel "Chewcifer" Walker

Jeffery Austin

Luke Carter

Molly Antimon

Erik Pineapple Martinez

Andy M

David Nichols II

Wanetta Bass-Wilde

Jim Pahel

Rhiannon Vose

Kyle Ulshafer

Bryony Baxter

Jordan Gonyea

Jessie and Amanda Wilburn

Daniel "Dadstar" Thompson

Katerina McCoy

Jay A Miller

George and Patti Dacosta

William D. Medlock II

Jessy Meyer

Sean Gray

Rheanna Lynn Stelly

Robyn

Onorato Wolfe

Britt West

Jeff Galbraith "Frostbittn"

Rona Horn

Creepieprowlie

Cassy Much

Timothy Matthews

In London's heart, where shadows creep,
Five ancient temples, buried deep.
Whispered tales, in midnight's hour,
Of hidden power, of unseen bower.

Beneath the Thames, where waters flow,
Lies the first, shrouded below.
Guarded by silence, wrapped in mist,
Its secret waits, in time's own twist.

In alleys twisted, narrow, tight,
The second stands, veiled from sight.
Its walls speak not of mundane lore,
But of legends, myths, and more.

Where market's bustle meets the eye,
The third temple does quietly lie.
In plain sight yet unseen by most,
Holds a past, a spectral host.

'Neath ancient park, where ravens call,
The fourth temple stands, proud and tall.
A hidden door, a whispered rite,
Leads to knowledge, locked from light.

In catacombs, where echoes dwell,
The final temple guards its spell.
In darkness steep, where secrets keep,
Lies the power, ancient, deep.

Five keys to find, in London's soul,
To unlock a tale untold.
He who dares these depths to plumb,
Will find the truth, when all is done.

Beware the thirteenth day of Friday's name,
Whispers an old curse, no mere game.
A secret pact, a cosmic bind,
Between two gods, in shadows entwined.

"The Prime," master of the eternal wheel,
Met "The End Scribe," to fate they kneel.
Their words echo in the ancient tome,
On the thirteenth, their powers roam.

In the moon's pale gleam, beware their sight,
For their quill scrawls doom in the dead of night.
Each stroke a fate, a life ensnared,
In the tapestry of horrors they've prepared.

Heed this warning, hold it near,
The thirteenth Friday brings more than fear.
It's a day when the unseen walk,
And in whispered winds, the old gods talk.

On this cursed day, keep watchful eye,
For fate's shadow looms beneath the sky.
Remember the tale of the divine scribe,
For on the thirteenth, their forces imbibe.

So guard your heart, and mind the lore,
On Friday the thirteenth, the gods explore.
Their ancient magic, dark and profound,
In their whispered curse, fate is bound.

Baa, baa, black sheep,
Have you any wool?
Yes, sir, yes, sir,
Three bags full;
One for the master,
And one for the dame,
And one for the little boy
Who lives down the lane.

Baa, baa, dark sheep,
What lies in your eyes?
Deep, sir, deep, sir,
Where the shadow lies;
One for the silence,
And one for the screams,
And one for the keeper
Of your darkest dreams.

Baa, baa, lost sheep,
Why do you weep?
Cold, sir, cold, sir,
In secrets we keep;
One for the endless,
And one for the void,
And one for the horrors
That can't be destroyed.

Baa, baa, dread sheep,
What do you see?
Night, sir, night, sir,
It's coming for thee;
One for the whispers,
And one for the moan,
And one for the darkness
That gnaws at your bone.

In the olden days, by candle's flickering light,
A pinch of salt thrown left to right,
For when the crystals scatter and fall,
Beware, for shadows begin their call.

Spilled salt, a simple, careless act,
Yet in the realms unseen, a binding pact,
Each grain, a beacon in the night,
Drawing forth things that shun the light.

Whispers in the ancient halls speak,
Of salt as a shield, both strong and weak,
A line against the creeping dread,
But once broken, leads the dark to your bed.

Old tales tell of the salt's true role,
In the cosmic game, an unspoken toll,
To spill is to invite chaos' dance,
A slip, a risk, a dangerous chance.

For in each grain lies a secret power,
Guarding homes at the witching hour,
But scattered wide, the protection fades,
And into your life, darkness invades.

So when salt tumbles from your hand,
Remember the lore of the ancient land,
Throw a pinch over your left shoulder,
To keep you safe, as the nights grow colder.

In this simple act, rebalance the scales,
A moment's gesture that tells the tales,
Of olden magic, deep and vast,
In the simple salt, legends cast.

Three blind mice, three blind mice,
See how they run, see how they run,
They all ran after the farmer's wife,
Who cut off their tails with a carving knife,
Did you ever see such a sight in your life,
As three blind mice?

But why did they run so blindly bold?
In the dead of night, in the bitter cold,
What secrets there lie untold,
About the mice, so brave and old?

Whispers tell in hushed tones low,
Of a curse that was cast long ago,
A farmer's pact with shadows' woe,
That left the mice in endless throe.

Their sight they lost, but gained a sense,
Of things beyond the mortal fence,
In darkness, yet their world immense,
A labyrinth of consequence.

The farmer's wife, with blade so keen,
Was not what she truly seemed,
A guardian of the line between,
The waking world and that unseen.

Her knife did sever more than tails,
In a saga of tragic tales,
A balance where the scale prevails,
In a world where light oft pales.

So when you hear their pitter-patter,
In the alleys, in the clatter,
Know the truth behind the matter,
It's more than just rodent chatter.

Three blind mice, now spirits roam,
In moonlit streets, their ghostly home,
Forever in twilight's dome,
They run, seeking what they've never known.

Take a coin and keep it close,
Making sure the head's opposed,
For when the time to bargain comes,
Silver never comes undone.

In the shadow of the moon,
Whisper low a cryptic tune,
Spin the coin thrice around,
Let it fall without a sound.

As it rests upon the ground,
Ancient spirits gather 'round,
For a coin of silver bright,
Holds the power of the night.

Speak your wish, but pay the price,
Silver demands a sacrifice,
For what's gained is never free,
Bound to a cosmic decree.

The coin's face, a gateway sealed,
In its flip, your fate's revealed,
Heads for fortune, tails for dread,
In the balance, hang the threads.

When the bargain is complete,
Take your leave, be discreet,
For the spirits, once conjured, stay,
Lingering in the light of day.

Guard the coin, keep it near,
A talisman of hope and fear,
In its metal, mysteries reside,
Silver's secret, deep inside.

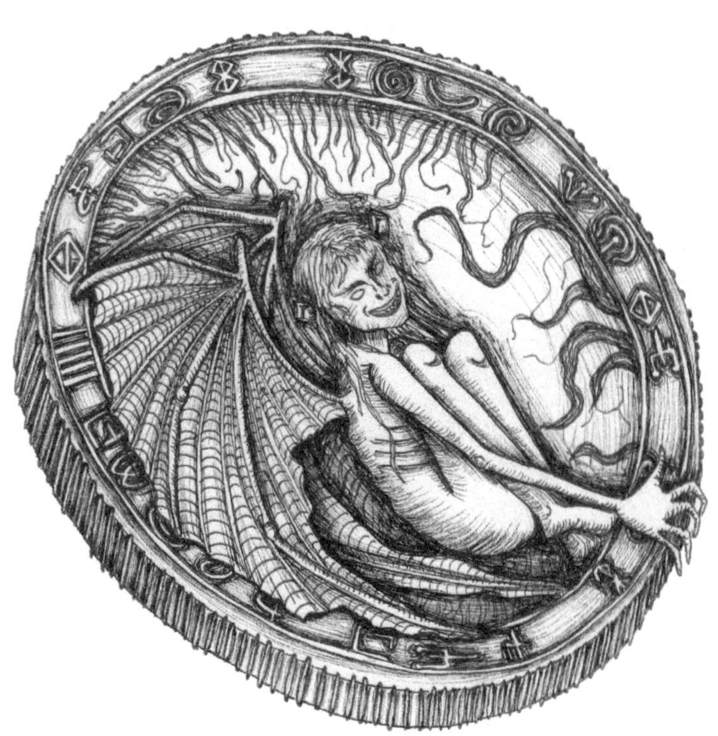

A Riddle

In ancient stone, where echoes stay,
A sacred place where time remains,
With pillars tall and whispers old,
Secrets lie within its fold.

No doors to lock, no key to find,
Yet wisdom's voice within confined,
Where spirits dwell and prayers ascend,
What is this place, where journeys end?

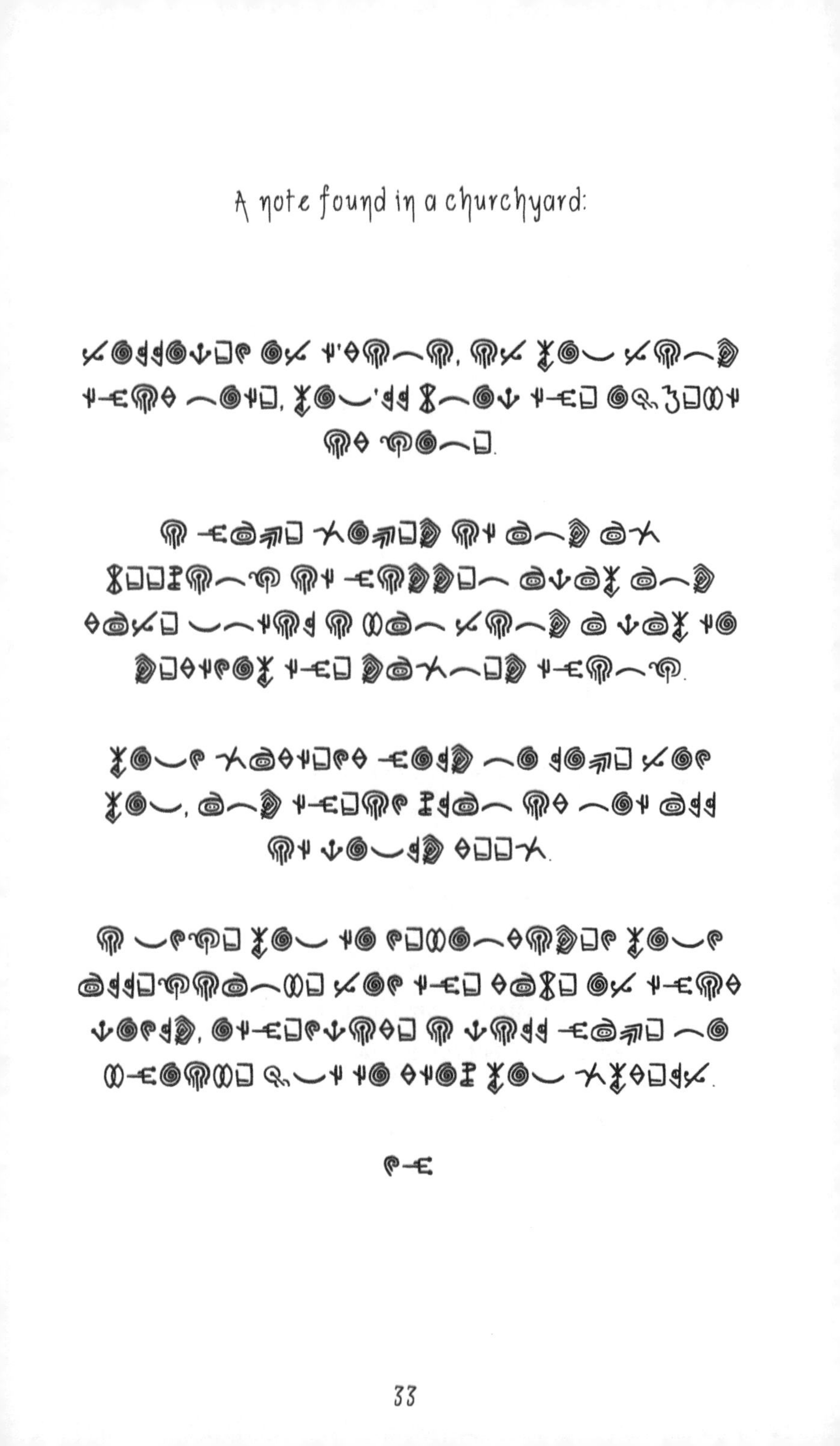

A note found in a churchyard:

Break a mirror, shatter glass,
And you may have looked your last.

Seven years of twisted fate,
In each shard, the shadows wait.

Every fragment, every sliver,
Holds a glimpse of the river,

Where time flows in reverse,
Bearing down an ancient curse.

In the glass, a realm unseen,
Lurks behind the silver sheen,

Echoes of a hidden face,
Trapped in time's unyielding space.

Look too deep, and you might find,
Secrets of a darker kind,

Whispers from the other side,
In the mirror's fractured tide.

So heed the tale of broken view,
For the myths may well be true,

In the mirror's splintered cast,
Lies a window to the past.

Step on a line,
Make a splinter in time.
Step on a crack
And you must never look back.

Cross a seam in the ground,
Hear a whispering sound.
Tread on a gap,
Fall into a trap.

Step in a groove,
Watch the world oddly move.
Walk on a split,
Into the unknown, you're lit.

Stride over a rift,
Feel reality shift.
Leap over a line,
Cross into a design.

Trace the cracks on the floor,
Open a forbidden door.
Follow each crease,
Discover a piece.

Venture with silent tread,
Into realms unsaid.
For where lines converge,
Secrets do emerge.

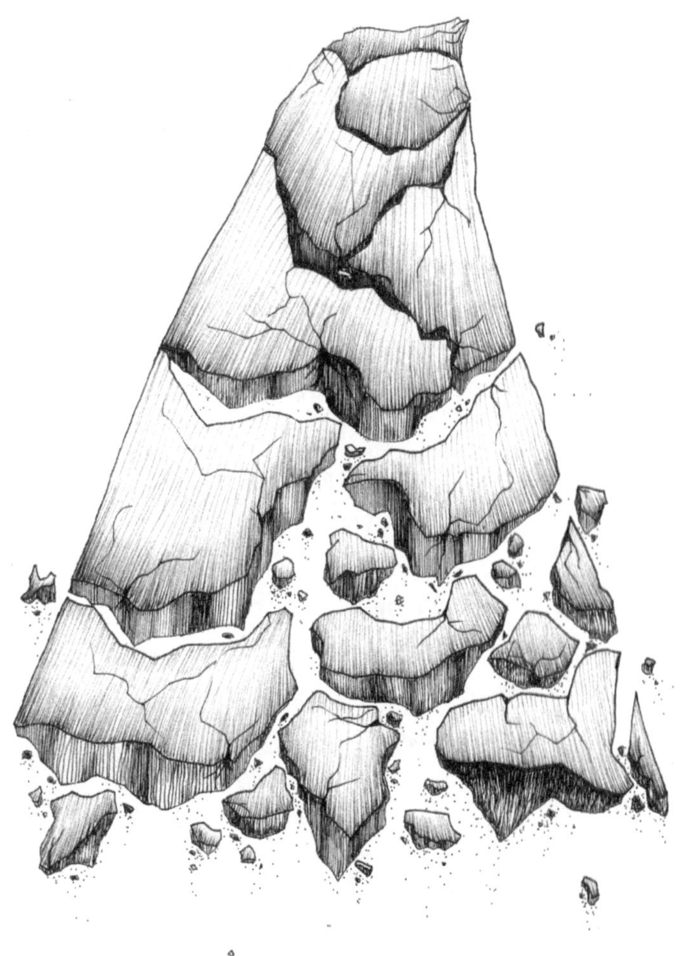

Cross your fingers, hold them tight,
In daylight's joy, in dread of night,
But do you know the ancient rite,
That hides within this simple sight?

In times of old, when myths were born,
When magic's breath and beasts forlorn,
Roamed the earth in twilight's morn,
Crossed fingers were a sign, not scorn.

Two paths entwined, like serpents' dance,
To summon luck, to change the chance,
To guard against a sidelong glance,
Of beings lurking in the expanse.

For in this gesture, secrets lie,
A pact with forces, shy and sly,
That weave the fabric of the sky,
And hold the answers, deep and high.

Yet heed this warning, clear and true,
The crossing is a gateway, too,
A door to realms, both old and new,
Where entities beyond pursue.

So when you cross in hopeful plea,
Remember what you cannot see,
The ancient bond, the silent key,
Between the worlds, the mystery.

For every wish and every dream,
That through crossed fingers, softly gleam,
Are heard by more than they may seem,
In shadows deep, where secrets teem.

Cross your fingers, if you dare,
But be aware of what you share,
For in this world, so foul and fair,
Crossed paths lead to the cosmic lair.

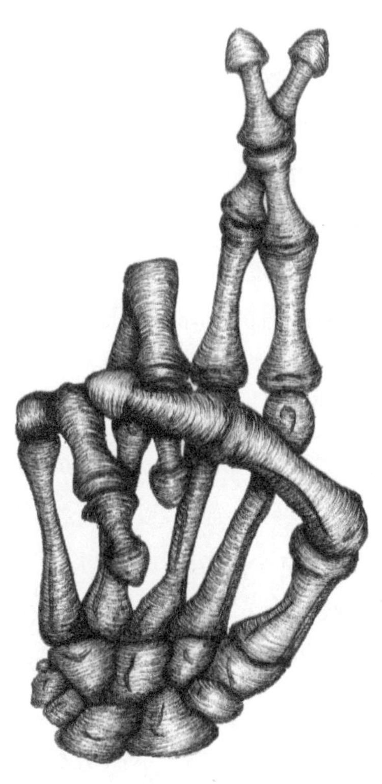

22nd September, 1872

The mist clings to the ground today, heavier than I have ever seen. It seems as though the very air carries the weight of our sins, a burden too great for this village to bear. I cannot shake the feeling that something dark watches from the shadows, lurking just beyond the edge of sight.

They have chosen. My heart aches, and yet, I knew it would come to this. I was just a girl the last time, but I still remember the villagers whispering the ancient chant and offering one of our own to the darkness that haunts the village. The elders say the ritual is the only way to keep the malevolent force at bay, but it does not make it any easier to accept. Today, it is my son, Samuel.

God forgive me, but I almost wish it had been another's child. But no, how could I? How could any mother wish this upon another? Yet, the thought lurks in the deepest recesses of my mind, a poisonous seed planted by desperation. I am ashamed. Samuel is so young, so full of life. He trusts me completely, and it is that trust that will lead him to his fate.

The villagers gathered at our door before the sun had fully risen, their faces stern and unyielding. Samuel was still asleep, his small body curled under the blankets. I wished, for a moment, to let him sleep forever, to spare him what was to come. But the knock came again, louder this time, and I knew I could not delay.

We walked together to the well. The others followed, silent as ghosts, their faces pale in the dim light of dawn. I held Samuel's hand, his small fingers wrapped around mine, warm and trusting. He asked where we were going, and I could not bring myself to answer.

The words of the chant began as we neared the well, old voices murmuring the ancient rhyme that has been passed down through generations.

By the blood of our kin
and the bones in the earth,

The ground beneath us seemed to tremble with each step. I could feel the presence stirring, as if it recognised the offering we were about to make.

Samuel looked up at me with wide, innocent eyes, and for a moment, I faltered. I wanted to snatch him up, to run as far as my legs could carry me. But I stood frozen, a prisoner of duty and fear. The mist thickened around us, swirling like a living thing, reaching out from the well towards my boy.

I whispered to him to be brave, my voice breaking as the tendril of mist wrapped around his small body. His eyes met mine one last time, full of confusion and fear. And then, he was gone, taken by the darkness that feeds on our despair.

The village is quiet now, too quiet. The others have returned to their homes, leaving me alone with my grief. Samuel's room is as we left it this morning, his toys scattered on the floor, his bed still warm. I sit on the edge, clutching his favourite blanket, the scent of him still clinging to the fabric.

How do I live with this? How do I continue on in a world where my child is no more? The others say that the sacrifice has bought us safety for another cycle, but I do not feel safe. I feel empty, hollowed out by the loss, by the knowledge that we will have to do this again.

I can still hear the chant, the words echoing in my mind.

Old gods of the deep,
of the night,
of the dread,

The mist outside my window curls and twists, as if it is alive, a reminder that the dark presence is never truly gone. It waits, patient and hungry, knowing that it will be fed again in time.

I wish to believe that this will end, that one day the village will be free of this curse. But in my heart, I know the truth. This is a place of darkness, and we are its prisoners. Our only choice is whom to sacrifice next.

God forgive us all.

The first is a storm where dark clouds loom,
Whispering of a world in gloom.

The second, lightning cuts the sky,
A tempest dance, wild and high.

The third brings hail, cold and fierce,
Nature's drumbeat, piercing and terse.

The fourth, a gale that churns the sea,
Waves in tumult, wild and free.

The fifth, a vortex spinning fast,
Spiralling winds, a furious blast.

The sixth, at night, as shadows play,
Thunder rolls, dark and fey.

The seventh, squalls lash the land,
Rain like tears, a sodden hand.

The eighth, snow blinds, a white embrace,
A blizzard's cold and icy face.

The ninth, pure fury, nature's roar,
Unleashed, untamed, a mythic lore.

The tenth, the end, skies torn apart,
Apocalypse, a broken heart.

The North Wind doth blow,
And we shall have snow,
And what will poor robin do then, poor thing?

He'll sit in a barn,
And keep himself warm,
And hide his head under his wing, poor thing.

But as the winds wail,
And the stars grow pale,
In the snow, there's a deeper chill, unseen.

For beyond the veil,
Where night skies sail,
Lies a realm where no mortal's been.

The robin, so small,
Feels the ancient call,
Of whispers old, and secrets dire.

In the heart of the storm,
Where shadows form,
Burns a hidden, cosmic fire.

The barn, once safe, once warm,
Transforms in the swarm,
Of snowflakes that dance with glee.

Each a sigil, a sign,
Of a lineage, divine,
An eldritch truth, a key.

And the robin, in fear,
Feels the end is near,
As the barn dissolves, a spectral sight.

In the eye of the wind,
Where dreams rescind,
The bird glimpses the cosmic night.

For the North Wind knows,
As it eternally blows,
A secret, dark and deep.

That beneath our world's face,
Lies another space,
Where old gods wake and creep.

So when the snow falls thick,
And the clock ticks quick,
Remember the robin's fate.

In the heart of the gale,
Lies a timeless tale,
Of a world beyond our gate.

Old King Cole was a merry old soul,
And a merry old soul was he;
He called for his pipe, and he called for his bowl,
And he called for his fiddlers three.

Every fiddler he had a fiddle,
And a very fine fiddle had he;
Oh, there's none so rare, as can compare,
With King Cole and his fiddlers three.

But in the night, where shadows creep,
And the world lies still, in slumber deep,
Old King Cole no longer sleeps,
For in his court, a darkness seeps.

The fiddlers three, with bows of bone,
Play tunes of madness, all alone,
Their melodies, in twilight zone,
Whisper secrets, in an undertone.

For King Cole's mirth was but a mask,
To hide the truth, a dreadful task,
In his bowl, a starlit flask,
Holding horrors, none would ask.

His pipe did smoke the smoke of fear,
Its fumes, a mist, both thick and clear,
And those who heard, could barely hear,
The otherworldly song so near.

In his kingdom, lost to time,
Each note played is a chilling chime,
Revealing truths of a sinister kind,
Of a universe, in its prime.

So heed the tale of Cole, once merry,
Whose laughter hid something scary,
In his realm, where shadows tarry,
Lies a truth, most extraordinary.

For in the depths of night's embrace,
King Cole's court is a haunted place,
Where fiddles play with ghastly grace,
A cosmic dance, a chilling race.

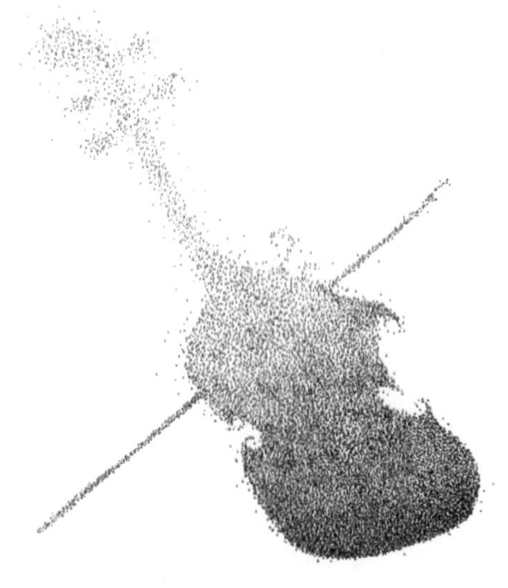

A Riddle

It dances lightly on the air,
A whispered touch, beyond compare,
No form to see, no hands to hold,
Yet it can warm you when you're cold.

It speaks in tones both high and low,
A language only hearts may know,
It lifts you up, or brings you down,
A king with neither throne nor gown.

It lives within both joy and pain,
A fleeting sound, a sweet refrain,
What moves the soul with unseen might,
And fills the world with pure delight?

A Riddle

Invisible thread that guides the way,
Beyond the night, beyond the day,
It shapes the path you're meant to take,
No matter the choices you may make.

It whispers soft or shouts aloud,
Through sunlit skies or under cloud,
Unseen hands that weave the tale,
Where dreams may soar or plans may fail.

It weaves through time, both swift and slow,
In every step, it makes us grow,
A force that's felt but never seen,
That's guided all the paths we've been.

Thirty days hath September,
April, June, and November,
All the rest have thirty-one,
Except February, twenty-eight days clear,
And twenty-nine in each leap year.

But hark, there lies a hidden time,
A month unspoken in the rhyme,
Where shadows twist and stars align,
In this lost month, the dark divine.

In this month, the thirteenth one,
The veil between worlds comes undone,
A realm where sun nor moon doth run,
And eldritch whispers weigh a ton.

This month, known to a haunted few,
Where ancient gods sip morning dew,
Their horrid forms in darkness stew,
In twisted realms of ghastly hue.

Here, time and space doth warp and bend,
Reality breaks, and rules amend,
The cosmic horrors, they descend,
On paths where stars and nightmares blend.

But fear not the month that never shows,
For in its absence, safety grows,
Yet in its essence, darkness knows,
The secrets of the deep cosmos.

So, heed the rhyme of months and days,
And walk not in the thirteenth's gaze,
For there, the ancient ones do laze,
In dreams beyond our mortal phase.

Thus ends the tale of time's dark maze,
Where hidden months hold older ways,
And whispered through the cosmic haze,
Are secrets of the end of days.

A New Year's resolution
is a pact you choose to make,
A silent promise to the stars,
a vow the heavens take.
In the stillness of the winter's night,
beneath the moon's cold gaze,
Each whispered goal, a sacred rite,
in the celestial maze.

With every word, the cosmos stirs,
an ancient power wakes,
A bond formed in the quiet hours,
where destiny shapes and shakes.
It's more than mere intention cast;
it's a dance with destinies vast,
A contract signed in frost's cold breath,
a dance with shadow, life, and death.

As clock hands join to greet the year,
in the realm where time is king,
Your hopes and fears, whispered near,
to otherworldly beings cling.
They weave your words into the sky,
where both dreams and darkness fly,
A tapestry of fate and chance,
in the universal expanse.

So choose your words with care and thought, under
the watchful eye of night,
For in the cosmic web they're caught,
bathed in the pale moonlight.
Remember, as you set your aim,
in this yearly, timeless game,
A New Year's pact, once freely made,
in eternity's memory is forever laid.

You know Dasher and Dancer
And Prancer and Vixen,
Comet and Cupid
And Donder and Blixem.

But have you forgotten the ancient lore,
Of the olde reindeer that came before?

Gloomhoof, the shadowed, with eyes like coal,
Roams in the night where the north winds blow.

Frostmane, the silent, with breath so cold,
Freezes the hearts of the brave and bold.

Nightwing, the swift, a spectre in air,
Glides through darkness, a phantom of despair.

Stormrage, the fierce, with thunderous might,
His eyes flash lightning in the deep of night.

Shadowhart, the elusive, who whispers the wind,
In the darkest of woods he makes the night sing.

Ironhoof, the ancient, with a gaze so stern,
His steps cause the earth itself to churn.

Ember-eye, the fire-bringer, with a burning glare,
Scorches the skies with a fiery flare.

Wraithbell, the sorrowful, with a mournful cry,
His presence brings clouds to a clear night sky.

Together they roam, in the darkest of nights,
A legion of shadows, ancient reindeer of frights.
So remember their names, and the tales of yore,
For they wander the earth, forevermore.

Recipe: Elixir of the Silver Veil

In the hour when the moon hides its face, and shadows dance with unseen whispers, gather the following with reverence and caution:

- **Essence of Nightshade**: Plucked at the stroke of midnight, when its power is most potent. Three drops are required, no more, no less.

- **A Raven's Feather**: Stolen from the left wing of a raven who has seen the passing of seven winters. Burn this feather until naught but ash remains, then add it to the cauldron.

- **Moonlit Dew**: Collected under the light of a waning crescent, from a place where no human has tread for a hundred years. Two teaspoons will suffice.

- **Crushed Bone of the Unseen**: Ground to a fine powder, this must be taken from a creature that walks between worlds. The bone must be cleansed with the tears of the forsaken before use. One pinch only.

- **The Breath of the Sleeping**: Capture it in a crystal vial on the night of a new moon. Allow no other air to taint its purity. This breath is to be released into the mixture at the very end, as the final ingredient.

Prepare a fire of cold flames, feeding it with the wood of the elder tree. Stir the concoction thrice anticlockwise with a silver spoon, then twice clockwise. As the last breath is released into the cauldron, speak these words but once, under your breath, lest the spirits overhear:

"Through shadow and smoke,
Reveal what is cloaked."

Let the elixir cool under the night sky, away from prying eyes. When the surface stills, the potion is complete. Drink with care, and may the silver veil lift for you alone.

Be Warned:

The path ahead is not always as it seems.

In the twisted grove where shadows play,
A silent watcher bides its stay.
Hidden 'neath the ancient tree,
A knower of things that should not be.

It speaks in tongues of elder times,
Each word a bell of chilling chimes.
Its sight pierces through the veil,
Of futures written in detail.

Dare you speak to that which waits,
Behind a veil of fae gates?
Its counsel deep, a venom's kiss,
Clad in the guise of promised bliss.

Its roots are steeped in blood-soaked lore,
Its branches scratch at heaven's door.
A serpent's coil, a spider's web,
In its gaze, the world's ebb.

Whispers weave into your mind,
A tapestry of fate unkind.
With every truth it so imparts,
A darker seed in your heart starts.

Flee the glade, ignore the call,
Of the one that sees, predicts, enthrals.
For once its visions in you burn,
There's no return, no overturn.

So children heed this fearsome rhyme,
Keep to the light and bide your time.
For in the dark, the truths you seek,
May be the end of the brave and meek.

An excerpt copied from an organist's diary:

There's a music in the silence, and I prefer the quiet of the Albert Hall at night. The after echo of the thousands of concert goers from whatever event was on today, it's like they leave an image behind, a silent whisper of ten-thousand souls. It breathes with me, that poised, energised silence, as I watch the shadows shift like old friends. Then I press the first key on the organ and the power erupts from the ten thousand pipes, shattering the silence. No, not quite shattering, but entering its space, mingling, mixing, commanding it. The chill in the air fills me and as I lift my finger from the cold, solid key the sound from the pipes seems to hang in the dark, waiting. It compels me.

I must continue my work. I know this piece I'm crafting is my magnum opus, it just feels... different from anything I've written before. It's hard to explain, and you wouldn't understand anyway, but there's something holy about it. Each note is a prayer, each chord feels like a step closer to something deeper, something ancient. The others assure me I'm on the right track. I've seen the eager looks in their eyes when they've been lucky enough to hear me working.

The hunger. I can barely remember starting, they just said this piece would be the key, they never said why or to what. A ritual of some kind? None of that seems to matter now. Sometimes I'm interrupted in my playing by one of the cleaners coming into the hall in the morning and I realise I must have been playing all night. I'm not sure I even remember it, I just... play. It's like I no longer know where I end, and the music begins.

I slip back into the music, a familiar old friend now, yearning to be known. I know I am close, that my master work is almost complete. As I play the shadows flicker in the corners of my eye, there's no breeze, no one passing by, just me and the music as my guide. The notes seem to stretch out into the gloom, echoing for just a fraction too long, almost as if something is starting to play them back to me. I barely notice my fingers as they glide over the keys, it's as if they're made of smoke. Have they always been this long?

My hands move instinctively up to the Great Organ for the climax of the work. As the chords erupt from the enormous, monstrously beautiful machine; twisting and coercing the air around them, the air seems to thicken and I feel eyes on me. But not the usual kind. They've been waiting for this. So have I. I'm filled with an urgent excitement and I am propelled forwards, onwards. My hands are a blur as they fly around the keys and I am merely a puppet to her whims.

We can hear the music, it is in us, we are building up to a cadence, and this feels like the one. The sound erupts in wave after wave of chaos and I cannot see the organ anymore, the hall seems to crumble away. The last chord hangs in the air and fades. But I can still hear it. A voice: soft, cold, mesmerising and perplexing whispers to me from the shadows...

"It is finished."

"Don't bite the hand that feeds you,"
as the old wisdom imparts,
For gratitude breeds harmony,
and kindness fills all hearts.
Yet remember, every hand that gives
can also take away,
In the balance of give and take,
our true characters display.

But what of hands that feed with shadows,
cloaked in deceit's guise?
Offering sustenance laced with lies,
under the guise of being wise.
Beware the giver whose gifts ensnare,
in silken chains that bind,
A sinister feast, where the benevolent beast,
reveals a darker mind.

In the depths of whispered corridors,
Where secrets fester and brood,
Lurks the hand that feeds with malice,
in a dangerous interlude.
A hand that giveth can also curse,
With a touch as cold as night,
Feeding not for love, but control,
veiled in deceptive light.

Such hands weave a web of control,
With every morsel they provide,
A game of chess with human pawns,
in the shadows they reside.
For every bite you take, a piece of self,
you might unknowingly yield,
In the twisted game, where the hand that feeds,
forces you to the field.

So heed this lesson, not just in thanks,
but in cautious discern,
For the hand that feeds can be the hand,
from which one must learn.
Beneath the cloak of charity,
sometimes hide intentions spurned,
And in biting not the hand, perhaps,
it's our own freedom earned.

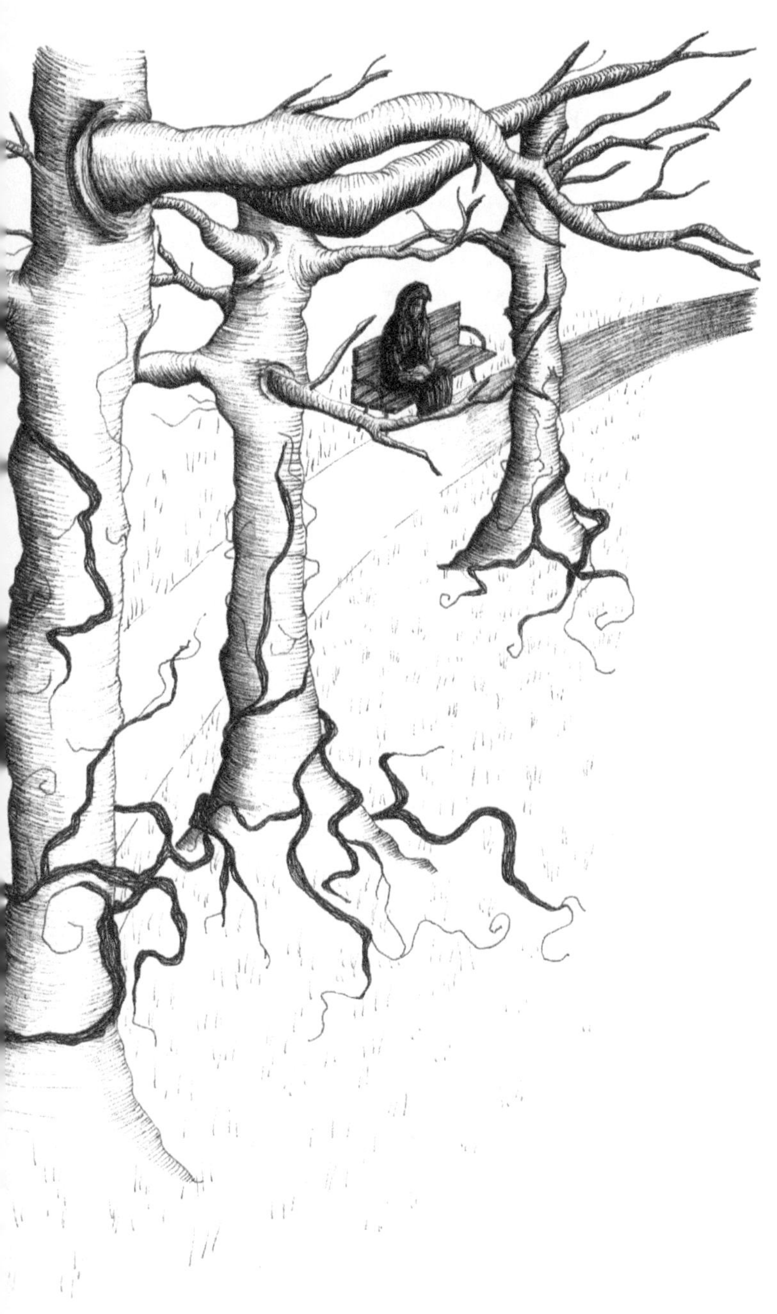

"Don't judge a book by its cover,"
a wise old saying goes,
For within the plainest bindings,
the richest story flows.
Look beyond the surface,
Where deeper truths reside,
In every unassuming page,
a world may hide inside.

But tread with care through hidden lore,
for not all tales are kind,
Some books, they breathe with ancient scripts,
with mysteries entwined.
In dusty shelves and shadowed nooks,
forgotten tomes may lie,
Whispering secrets in the dark,
under a moonless sky.

Each page a door to realms unknown,
Where eerie silence reigns,
Words twist like serpents, in cryptic dance,
binding with unseen chains.
The air grows thick, the walls close in,
as you turn each page with dread,
In hidden ink, the cursed truths
of a world unsaid.

What starts as curiosity,
can end in fateful snare,
Each chapter a deeper descent
into the lair of despair.
For books are more than paper and ink,
they hold powers unseen,
In their embrace, reality bends,
and nightmares blend with dream.

So when you choose to crack a spine,
and peer into its heart,
Remember, some knowledge is a curse,
a venomous, dark art.
For within the pages of some books,
there lurk terrors untold,
And by their cover, you'll never guess
the horrors they may hold.

Many hands make light work,
in unity they find strength,
Joined in common purpose,
their power grows at length.
In the tapestry of toil,
each thread intertwines,
Together they build wonders,
as harmony designs.

Yet, beneath this unity,
a darker truth does hide,
Many hands in shadows,
where secrets do reside.
With each twist and turn,
their motives intertwine,
A pact made in silence,
beneath the moon's pale shine.

In the hush of twilight,
where whispers weave the air,
Hands that once brought daylight
now clasp in grim despair.
Eldritch chants are murmured,
as stars begin to blink,
Binding ancient forces
on the eternal brink.

Through the veils of darkness,
their true work unfolds,
Crafting not just wonders,
but stories left untold.
An altar of ambition,
Where fates are intertwined,
In the grip of many hands,
destiny's redesigned.

So beware the many,
When they move as one,
For in their silent unity,
a darker deed is done.
In the harmony of shadows,
Where hidden truths embark,
Many hands make light work,
but also conjure the dark.

Strike while the iron is hot,
in fervour and in thought,
Seize the moment's chance,
lest it be for naught.
For when the fire cools,
opportunities are lost,
Act with swift resolve,
regardless of the cost.

Beneath the glowing forge,
Where shadows dance and weave,
Lies a hidden realm,
Where the restless spirits grieve.
Each hammer's strike a call,
to powers deep and old,
Echoing in the dark,
Where secrets dare unfold.

In the heart of flame,
Where earthly rules distort,
Lurk whispers of a pact,
in the infernal court.
What once was wrought in steel,
now bound by eerie lore,
Bargains forged in fire,
With the spectral core.

The anvil holds more
than just metal's fate,

It's a portal to a realm,
Where dark forces congregate.
Each glowing piece that's shaped,
With pounding, rhythmic beat,
Awakens something ancient,
stirring in the heat.

In this fearful dance,
of fire, iron, and air,
The forger's soul entwines
With a power stark and bare.
For every item made,
a sliver of essence caught,
In the realm beyond the flame,
Where reality is naught.

As the fire dims,
and shadows reclaim their throne,
The forger senses truths,
to mortal minds unknown.
In the cooling metal,
secrets eternally hot,
Bound within the iron,
by a fate long sought.

So, heed the age-old warning,
in the forging plot,
Strike while the iron is hot,
but fear what cannot be forgot.

Two little dickie birds sitting on a wall,
One named Peter, one named Paul.
Fly away Peter! Fly away Paul!
Come back Peter! Come back Paul!

Two little dickie birds floating through air,
One came home and one isn't there.
"Where is Peter?" Cried out Paul,
But Peter wasn't ever really there at all.

Two little dickie birds flying through the night,
Ones lost forever, vanished from sight.
Paul, all alone, searched high and low,
But shadows whispered secrets he shouldn't know.

Two little dickie birds now just a dream,
One lost to darkness, the other to a scream.
Echoes of Peter haunt the silent wall,
And Paul's reflection no longer answers his call.

A penny for your thoughts,
dear child of the night,
In the gloaming where
shadows and secrets alight.
Beyond the edge of reality,
Where old magicks reside,
There's a tale to be told,
and a truth to hide.

A penny, they say,
With a glint and a gleam,
Can unlock the dark vaults
of a long-forgotten dream.
For in the time of ancients,
When the World was still young,
A sorcery was born,
a dark song to be sung.

Tarnished and worn,
in a whisper it calls,
To those who would listen,
to the echo in the halls.
A thought for a penny,
a memory to share,
But with it comes a burden,
a darkness to bear.

For the coin has a power,
an old magic within,
To draw forth the shadows,
the sinners and the sin.
One might glimpse futures,
or secrets long past,
But the cost is your soul,
in its icy grasp.

A penny for your thoughts,
a dangerous game to play,
For once the truth's known,
it can never fade away.
The memories and nightmares,
the joy and the pain,
All dance in the mind,
an eternal refrain.

The old witches knew it,
the alchemists too,
That a coin could hold magic,
dark and true.
A circlet of metal,
so simple and small,
Yet within its curve,
the power to enthral.

So next time you're tempted,
by a whisper or glance,
To offer your thoughts
for a mere coin's chance.
Remember the legends,
the stories of old,
Of the penny's dark magic,
and the truths it once told.

Something old,
Something new,
Something borrowed,
Something blue.

Something gleaming, from the deep,
Where the merfolk softly weep.
Something fiery, plucked from night,
Where stars burn with eerie light.

Something shadowed, from a dream,
Whispers of a ghostly scream.
Something crimson, like the moon,
On the darkest night of June.

Something twisted, from the wood,
Where the ancient spirits stood.
Something golden, from a crypt,
Where old curses softly slipped.

Something silver, from the sky,
Where the astral dragons fly.
Something gleaming, like a jewel,
Stolen from a sorcerer cruel.

Something cold, from winter's grip,
Where the frost sprites lightly skip.
Something echoed, a mournful cry,
From a phoenix, set to die.

Something timeless, from the ages,
Found within forgotten pages.
Something whispered, secrets bound,
In a tongue, long un-found.

Something silent, from the void,
Realms that mankind once avoided.
Something humming, a mystic rune,
Summoning a spectral tune.

Gather these, in dark's embrace,
At the crossroad's haunted space.
With a chant and rite decreed,
The ancient one shall be freed.

Twinkle, twinkle, little star,
How I wonder what you are!
Up above the world so high,
Like a diamond in the sky.

Twinkle, twinkle, fading light,
Hiding secrets, cosmic fright.
Beyond the void, a pulsing glare,
Ancient beings, worlds despair.

Twinkle, twinkle, star of doom,
Whispering of our impending gloom.
Guardian of the cosmic gate,
Where timeless horrors lie in wait.

Within your glow, the abyss stirs,
Ancient chants, the universe blurs.
Twinkle, twinkle, star so far,
Bearing witness to our final hour.

It's said a god had a design
the fairies didn't like,
A tapestry of shadow,
Woven through the night.
With threads of dark desires,
the cosmos she would weave,
But light-hearted fairies
schemed beneath the eaves.

They danced upon the winds,
their laughter silver bells,
Plotting in the twilight
to disrupt her darkened spells.
With every stitch the god would place,
they'd counter with a gleam,
Their luminescence sowing seeds
of light within her dream.

The battle raged in whispers,
in the fabric of the skies,
Where stars watched in silence,
hidden from mortal eyes.
The god, with anger burning,
struck the firmament with might,
While fairies, quick and daring,
dodged in fleets of light.

Their clash, a symphony of chaos,
resounding through the void,
Where the aurora borealis was born,
and peace destroyed.
The energy immense,
it cracked through time and space,
Leaving trails of vibrant hues
the dark could not erase.

Now, when the sky turns
to its deepest, darkest blue,
The northern lights emerge,
in dazzling shades of hue.
A reminder of the battle,
of the fight to keep the night,
Where fairies danced against a god
to gift us with the light.

So, if you find yourself beneath
the eerie, mystic glow,
Remember the ancient struggle
from many eons ago.
For in the beauty of the aurora,
with its curtains softly drawn,
Lies a war of light and shadow,
that forever will go on.

The Eternal field
Trees of Timeless Twilight

Meeting Point

Golden Arch

A Choice

Pit of Punishment

The Midnight Forest

When the clock strikes the midnight hour,
And the world sleeps under night's bower,
A whistle blows, distant and faint,
Announcing the arrival of the Midnight Train.

It comes from nowhere, yet everywhere,
Its tracks unseen, in the cool night air,
Its carriages shrouded in misty veil,
On a timeless journey, without a trail.

Its conductor, a shadow, tall and thin,
Invites you aboard with a knowing grin,
"All aboard for destinations unknown,"
He calls, in a deep, reverberating tone.

Passengers few, with eyes wide and bright,
Embark on the train in the dead of night,
Seeking adventure, or running from fate,
Their stories untold, their future a slate.

The train glides silently, through realms unseen,
Through starlit skies and fields of green,
Past cities forgotten, and rivers of dreams,
Under the moon's soft, silvery beams.

Where it goes, no one can say,
For the journey changes, night to day,
Each trip unique, a path anew,
Through dimensions where the cold winds blew.

Some say it travels to yesterday,
To moments lost and times astray,
Others whisper of tomorrow's embrace,
Of uncharted worlds, in time and space.

But when dawn's light begins to creep,
The Midnight Train returns to sleep,
Vanishing as though it were never there,
Except in the hearts of those who dare.

So if you hear the whistle's cry,
Under the starry, velvet sky,
Will you board the Midnight Train,
And embark on a journey,
through the mystical domain?

We knock on wood, in hopeful tone,
To ward off ill, to set the stone,
But do you know, what lies beneath,
The grain, the bark, the hidden sheath?

In ancient woods, where shadows play,
And night outlasts the light of day,
There stand the trees, so old, so wise,
Guardians of our earth and skies.

Each knock we give, a plea, a rite,
A call within the darkest night,
But every tap, a price to pay,
For in the wood, the spirits sway.

They listen close, with ears unseen,
To promises and what they mean,
The wood remembers, holds the score,
Of all the knocks from days of yore.

The tree, it groans, it knows your fears,
Your hopes, your dreams, your hidden tears,
It holds them in its ancient core,
Each knock, a bond forevermore.

But beware the knock without respect,
A hollow sound, a false aspect,
For the spirits know, and they discern,
The truthful heart from one that spurns.

So when you knock, remember well,
The tales that ancient forests tell,
Of spirits old, and powers vast,
In wooden realms, where time has passed.

For every knock, a story told,
Of human fates, both bright and bold,
But heed the warning, clear and good,
Beware the spirit, "Knock on Wood."

In a house where whispers cling,
An umbrella's curse will sing.
Open it within these walls,
Tempt the fate that then befalls.

A shield 'gainst rain, 'gainst storm, 'gainst sky,
Lying quiet, waiting, dry.
Respect the guard of open air,
For inside, its powers snare.

Disrespect the guardian's role,
Unleash the shadows on your soul.
For nature's armour, used amiss,
Will invite a spectral kiss.

So heed the rule, old as the rain,
Keep closed that which shields the plain.
For in this act, a simple creed,
Respect the shield, respect its need.

In fields of green, where shadows play,
The Enigma sought to cloak in grey.
But fae danced under moonlit skies,
And left a gift of rare surprise.

Four leaves on clovers, hidden well,
Against the dark, a secret spell.
A few found here, and some found there,
Tiny wards that darkness dare.

Whisper soft, tread light and quick,
Each leaf is a candle's wick.
If found, hold tight to this small charm,
A four-leaf clover keeps from harm.

So sing this rhyme in twilight's hush,
Through clover fields in evening's blush.
Remember the luck these leaves bestow,
Guardians strong against the shadow.

A horseshoe that is made of iron,
Cast in the fires of dusk and dawn.
Hung above the old barn door,
Warding off the spirits of yore.
In its curve, a binding spell,
Iron grips the earth's raw knell.

A horseshoe that is made of silver,
Forged beneath a moonlit shiver.
Its gleam cuts through the shadow's heart,
A silent ward, a sacred art.
Beneath its arch, the night's mist dances,
Silver's light hides ancient chances.

A horseshoe that is made of gold,
Rich and warm, yet nobly old.
Kings and thieves covet its blaze,
Lustrous power in its gaze.
Round the curve, prosperity rings,
For gold summons the fortune it brings.

A horseshoe that is made of ash,
Whispered to from smoke and sash.
From trees where spirits whisper low,
It holds the secrets earth does know.
Hung where roots and dreams may meet,
Ash guides souls with silent feet.

A horseshoe that is made of lead,
Heavy with the words unsaid.
Shielding homes from storm and strife,
Lead absorbs the pains of life.
In its weight, a quiet force,
Guides the lost upon their course.

A Warning

In the shrouded mists of forgotten lore,
A whisper winds through the sycamore:
"Three omens dark shall mark thy days,
In their shadow, hide your gaze."

First, the raven, black as coal,
Shall cry thrice to take its toll,
Its call a knell that chills the bone,
For where it lands, luck has flown.

Next, the mirror, silver clear,
Cracks upon a fate most drear.
Its shattered face, a spider's web,
Casts futures dark with dread and ebb.

Lastly, comes the clock that chimes
At midnight in these haunted times,
Three tolls it sounds, not one note more,
To seal the fate that night has bore.

Beware, beware, the triad's thrall,
The ancient magic binds them all.
Each a piece of darker arts,
Weaving woe through human hearts.

For in this prophecy, old and grim,
Lies a truth, stark and dim:
Bad luck's trio, not mere chance,
But threads pulled in destiny's dance.

Heed this warning, keep it near,
Or fall to shadows, gripped by fear.
The old magic knows your tread,
Threefold curse upon your head.

A Riddle

A drop of me can change your fate,
I'm sweet or bitter on your plate,
I hide in colours bright and bold,
Yet in my grip, the heart turns cold.

I dance within a tempting glass,
Or linger in the sweetest mass,
In whispered words, in silent sighs,
I bring an end without goodbyes.

What am I, that lurks unseen,
In the fairest fruit, or darkest green?
A silent foe, a hidden sting,
What is the danger that I bring?

A Riddle

I'm found in clovers, so they say,
Or when the dice roll just your way,
I come and go without a sound,
In moments lost, or moments found.

I favour some, yet others shun,
A fickle dance that's never done,
In every game, in every chance,
I guide the hand, the coin's last glance.

I'm blamed in loss, and praised in gain,
A force unseen, both joy and pain,
I tip the scales, I sway the tide,
Yet none can say where I reside.

What am I, with fleeting grace,
That changes pace in every place?
A mystery wrapped in a fleeting touch,
What is this power we call so much?

Humpty Dumpty sat on a wall,
Humpty Dumpty had a great fall.
All the king's horses and all the king's men,
Couldn't put Humpty together again.

Humpty Dumpty now astray,
Lost in realms of disarray,
Where times undone and shadows play,
And sanity frays in the light of day.

The king's horses and the king's men,
Ventured beyond their mortal ken,
To bring Humpty back from the void's den,
They ventured into the eldritch glen.

In the maw of chaos they found their dread,
Where galaxies swirl and stars bled.
They glimpsed what lay in the abyss' bed,
And wished for sweet oblivion instead.

Humpty Dumpty once so small,
Became the nexus of it all.
In the cosmic echo of his fall,
We hear the universe's thrall.

All the king's horses and all the king's men,
Never returned home again.
Humpty echoes in their screams,
In a world beyond, where reality dreams.

If a cat of black doth cross your path,
Beware the scribe's dark, inky mark;
Eyes like voids, a silent hiss,
Marks the end with a spectral kiss.

Whiskers quiver in the moon's pale light,
Shadows dance in the heart of night;
Those who keep this feline near,
May escape the fate they fear.

But tread softly, speak not its name,
For the cat of night is no tame game;
In its fur lie secrets deep,
Guarding souls it's sworn to keep.

When the black cat crosses, time may bend,
As unseen forces, their wills extend;
Keep the darkness close, hold it tight,
To ward off the scribe's eternal night.

Out of sight, out of mind,
What, in the shadows, will you find?
Whispers lurking, ever near,
Breathing secrets, sowing fear.

Gone from view, but ever there,
In the stillness of the air;
Eyes unseen that watch you sleep,
In the dark, their vigil keep.

Forgotten voices, silent screams,
Haunt your steps and stalk your dreams;
Out of mind, but ever close,
Ghostly presences engross.

Where the unseen terrors hide,
In the corners, they abide;
Out of sight, but always here,
Whispering madness, drawing near.

In the deep and silent void,
Where shadows softly creep,
T'sini weaves her spectral loom
Within the realm of sleep.

Her fingers dance on threads of thought,
Where dreams and riddles twine,
A tapestry of shifting truths,
both mortal and divine.

Her voice, a haunting melody,
it echoes through the night,
A lullaby of labyrinths
Where wrong is never right.

Her song entangles waking minds
in webs of whispered lies,
A puzzle with no end or key,
beneath her moonlit eyes.

She weaves the veil of what is real,
of what may never be,
Her fabric flows like silken smoke,
unraveling mystery.

Through corridors of shifting walls,
Where echoes seem to speak,
The questions fold within themselves,
the answers hide and peek.

In mazes spun from dreams half-lost,
she watches as you stray,
Each corner hides a truth unknown,
each turn a night from day.

Reality becomes a riddle,
perception but a guise,
For T'sini smiles behind the mask,
a secret in disguise.

Her loom spins out the midnight thread,
where night and day collide,
And in her labyrinth of thoughts,
all certainties have died.

The Enigma reigns where reason fades,
where truth is but a breath,
In T'sini's world of woven lies,
there is no life or death.

So wander through her dream-bound halls,
where every path is new,
But know, dear soul, in T'sini's grip,
you'll never find what's true.

For she, the Mistress of the Maze,
delights in your despair,
As you unravel, piece by piece,
within her endless snare.

I'M FREE

I'm free

I'm free

I'M FREE

I'm free

I'M

I'm free

I'M FREE

I'm free I'm free I'm free I'm
free I'm free I'm free I'm free I'm
I'm free I'm free I'm free
free I'm free I'm free I'm free
I'm free I'm free I'm free I'm free I'm
I'm free I'm free I'm free
free I'm FREE

An excerpt from 'On What I've Lost'

Beware, beware the walker in the void,
Riskarr his name, in darkness deployed.
Where he treads, the stars do wane,
Bringing chaos, fear, and pain.

In the night sky, if his shadow falls,
Heed the warning, heed the calls.
For Riskarr brings a fearsome fate,
Entropy and terror, he'll create.

Avoid his path, stay clear, stay bright,
Lest you're lost in endless night.
Riskarr, the void where light does sink,
On his approach, the bravest shrink.

So guard your heart, keep your light,
Against the void, against the night.
For when Riskarr walks, the cosmos shakes,
And all that's sure, he might unmake.

What will be, will be
if it's written in the book,
A dark god's hand will etch your fate
with a single look.
His eyes are cold, his heart a void,
his soul a dreadful blight,
In shadows deep, he writes your doom
by dimming candlelight.

He sits alone, where whispers wail,
in halls made all of stone,
His writing quill a serpent's fang,
it carves through flesh and bone.
With every stroke, he binds a soul
to endless dying night,
In twisted paths of pain, they're trapped
where hope has taken flight.

He feasts on every fear,
delights in sorrow's endless flow,
Inventing the cruellest of fates
in the dim and murky glow.
There is no mercy in his gaze,
no kindness in his heart,
Just endless aching torment
spun from darkness, foul and tart.

Beware the silence of his pen,
for it has dreadful might,
For once your name is writ,
you cannot ever flee the night.
In his book of horrors,
your fate forever sealed,
To the dark god's cruellest whims,
your end is thus revealed.

What will be, will be,
the shadows softly sing,
As he writes your doom
beneath the moon's cold ring.

www.ingramcontent.com/pod-product-compliance
Lightning Source LLC
Chambersburg PA
CBHW030601310726
48979CB00003B/523

* 9 7 8 1 7 3 9 5 1 6 4 4 4 *